"Where Is the Earthling?" Asks a Strange Mechanical Voice.

It is the voice of a robot.

In a panic, you turn to the panel and push a purple button.

The section of floor on which you are standing begins to rise. Higher and higher you go. *I'll be crushed when I get to the ceiling,* you think.

Suddenly there is a loud pounding on the door. . . .

If you jump off the platform, turn to page 83.

If you think the platform may be a way out, turn to page 102.

But either way, you won't lose. Because if you don't like one ending, all you need to do is turn back a few pages to start the excitement all over again!

D0816024

WHICH WAY BOOKS for you to enjoy

Available from ARCHWAY paperbacks

WHICH WAY BOOKS #8

COSMIC ENCOUNTERS

R.G. Austin

ILLUSTRATED BY DOUG JAMIESON

AN ARCHWAY PAPERBACK
Published by POCKET BOOKS • NEW YORK

AN ARCHWAY PAPERBACK *Original*

An Archway Paperback published by
POCKET BOOKS, a Simon & Schuster division of
GULF & WESTERN CORPORATION
1230 Avenue of the Americas, New York, N.Y. 10020

ISBN: 0-671-45097-2

First Archway Paperback printing September, 1982

10 9 8 7 6 5 4 3 2 1

For Andrea, Eric, Rusty and Scott

Attention!

Which Way Books must be read in a special way. DO NOT READ THE PAGES IN ORDER. If you do, the story will make no sense at all. Instead, follow the directions at the bottom of each page until you come to an ending. Only then should you return to the beginning and start over again, making different choices this time.

There are many possibilities for exciting adventures. Some of the endings are good; some of the endings are bad. If you meet a terrible fate, you can reverse it in your next story by making new choices.

Remember: Follow the directions carefully and have fun!

You are an astronaut. After three years of training, you have learned how to control your heartbeat so that you will not age at the normal human rate. You have mastered the complex computers on the spacecraft. You have learned how to communicate by electrotelephonic waves. And you have studied intergalactic astronomy so that you will be able to recognize those planets that might harbor life.

Finally, you are ready for your first solo flight.

(continued on page 2)

The countdown begins: 10–9–8–7–6–5–4–3–2–1. Blastoff! The thrust of the solid-fuel rockets leaves magnificent plumes of yellow exhaust as you lift off from the surface of the Earth. In minutes, you have passed through the Earth's atmosphere into the zero-gravity vastness of outer space.

"Prepare to set your coordinates for the Olympus Galaxy," the woman at ground control says.

You follow her directions carefully.

(continued on page 3)

Suddenly, the spacecraft begins to tremble and the emergency lights flash. One of the solar fuel cells located on the tail of the ship has malfunctioned.

You decide to climb outside the module and repair the fuel cell.

(continued on page 5)

You attach a lifeline to the belt on your space suit. Then you climb through the portal.

Although you have practiced in simulated conditions on Earth, you are not prepared for the exhilarating feeling of zero gravity. You are weightless, just floating and flying in space.

Carefully, you make your way to the rear of the craft. You can see the solar fuel cell that is malfunctioning. It seems to have come loose from its connecting conduit.

Just as you reach for the cell to make the connection, the lifeline slips loose from your belt.

If you try to repair the cell and then crawl along the ship back to the portal, turn to page 10.

If you reach for the lifeline, turn to page 13.

"What is a Computerized Particle Decoder?" you ask.

"It will enable us to determine the makeup of Earthlings," the captain replies.

"But will it harm me?" you ask, terrified.

"It is our belief, based on scientific data, that it will not."

"But you have no proof?" you ask.

"None. We have never met an Earthling before. However, that makes no difference. You must do as you are ordered to do."

You have no choice.
Turn to page 26.

The object grows closer and closer. You keep thinking that it will change course, but it does not. The object moves directly toward you at an awesome speed. *This is it*, you think as you prepare to crash.

But there is no crash. Instead, you are simply swallowed up by the craft. You are astounded. *It never even slowed down*, you think.

Everything is silent. You seem to be trapped inside a giant void. You do not know where you are or what to do.

Then your portal opens, and you find yourself staring at three people who look exactly alike.

"Welcome," says one.

"Welcome," says the second.

"Welcome," says the third.

"Come with us," says one. The other two nod.

You have no choice.
Turn to page 20.

You are chilled and think that you would like the warmth of the hot spring. You walk in that direction.

When you reach the edge of the spring, you can feel the heat rising. The soupy substance is a thick orange-red, and it bubbles continuously. Occasionally, a bubble bursts and sprays tiny jets of the liquid into the air. A bubble bursts close to shore, and just one drop lands on your suit. You are horrified to see that it eats right through your clothes and burns your leg. You are standing by an acid lake!

You turn around and start to run. You bump directly into a massive rough and rubbery wall.

If you stop running and investigate the wall, turn to page 36.

If you keep on running and try to reach your spacecraft, turn to page 63.

"Are you certain you will not do it?" the captain asks.

"I am positive," you answer.

"Then you are useless," the captain replies. "Take the Earthling out of here."

You are dragged out of the control room to a door. It is opened and, without a word, you are thrown out.

You drift away into the space beyond.

The End

Fearfully, you watch your lifeline float away. Then you set about the task of repairing the solar fuel cell connection.

You are successful! Very carefully, always holding on to the ship, you make your way back to the portal and re-enter the ship.

You sit down at the control panel.

You are so exhausted from the task you have just completed that you fall asleep.

When you awaken, you look out. Your heart skips a beat when you realize that you are way off course, careening toward the unknown.

I have no choice, you think. *I must try to reverse course until I can locate my position.*

Turn to page 16.

You walk toward the noise. Something moves. You cannot believe your eyes. There, hunched before you, is a man! A thick layer of hair covers his body; an animal skin is wrapped around his waist. Even though he is fearsome to look at, he appears to be frightened and unsure of what or who you are.

"Gleek," he says.

You do not understand.

"Gleek, gleek, gleek," he says, pounding on his chest.

That must be his name, you think.

"Gleek," you say with a smile and hold out your hand.

"Gleek." He nods and grabs your arm.

If you shove Gleek away, turn to page 17.

If you lead Gleek to your spacecraft, turn to page 41.

You travel with the alien on a conveyor belt made of flexible metal. It takes you through a splendid, shining city that is spotlessly clean. The air is pure and the beings are polite. It is a wondrous place to be.

Just as you are being shown an example of the small spacecraft that is given to each family for private use, a huge trembling occurs. The entire planet shakes; the atmosphere turns dark.

When the trembling stops and the light returns, the alien speaks to you.

"Tragedy has struck our planet. For millions of years we have feared this, and now it has occurred. The planet has moved into a gaseous cloud that has changed the anti-matter gravitational field surrounding our planet into a permanent and impenetrable shield. We can no longer leave the planet; nor can any spacecraft enter our atmosphere. I fear that you will have to remain here for the rest of your days."

The End

You reach out to grab the lifeline and lose contact with the ship. The lifeline is just out of reach—and so is the ship.

Helplessly, you watch as the spacecraft continues on its journey without you.

I am doomed, you think as the craft becomes a small dot in the distance. You are alone in space.

Turn to page 18.

You take evasive action, turning first to your right, then to your left. Finally, using a circular maneuver, you manage to get away from the strange craft; but in doing so, you lose track of which way you are traveling.

In no time, you find yourself headed directly toward a small, dark planet.

At least it's not chasing me, you think, as you prepare to land.

When you step out of your spacecraft, you hear a strange, grunting noise.

If you investigate the noise, turn to page 11.

If you jump into your spacecraft and take off, turn to page 28.

"I don't want to go to a planet where there are no feelings. I won't strap myself in. I absolutely refuse," you say.

"Don't be a fool," says the man. "We will enter the atmosphere any second now and if you don't—"

Suddenly, there is a huge jolt as the ship enters the Conwa atmosphere. You lurch forward and receive a fatal blow to your head.

The End

You reverse course. But the longer you travel, the more confused you become.

Soon, you see a bright object through the porthole. It is heading directly toward you!

If you think it is wise to maintain course, turn to page 7.

If you try to take evasive action, turn to page 14.

Gleek stumbles. You run. But Gleek is faster than you. He reaches out his huge muscular arm, picks you up, and throws you over his shoulder. Then he carries you toward the mountains in the distance.

Strange animal cries fill the air and sputtering volcanoes cast a red glow in the sky. You feel as if you are being drawn back in time to the days of prehistory on Earth. And yet you know that you are on another planet with its own evolutionary past.

The road becomes steeper as you enter a terrain filled with rocks and valleys and cliffs. Finally, Gleek carries you through a small opening between two boulders and enters a hidden valley. Then he sets you down.

You see twelve other members of Gleek's tribe. They throw up their hands in shock and fear at the sight of you.

"It is all right," you say. "I will not harm you."

"Na! Ugh! Ugh! Na!" the people cry.

If you walk toward the people with your arm extended in friendship, turn to page 25.

If you think walking closer might be interpreted as a threat, turn to page 44.

You look into the vastness of the universe. The lights of distant stars sparkle.

Suddenly, you notice that one of the lights is moving toward you at an incredible speed. When it gets closer, you see red lights spinning crazily around the edges of a pancake-shaped vehicle. You are astounded. You did not know that ground control had prepared for such an emergency.

The rescue ship is enormous. It stops and hovers next to you. A shining silver door slides open and an automated arm is extended. You grab hold and are pulled into the ship.

Inside, three people, dressed in bizarre space suits, greet you.

"Thank goodness!" you say. "You've saved me! How did Mission Control do this so quickly?"

No one answers your question. Instead, they beckon you to follow them.

(continued on page 19)

You are taken through corridors of shining steel, then into an elevator. Although you ask questions as you walk, you receive no answers.

The elevator door opens, and you are overwhelmed at the size of the Control Room. It is vast. Overhead, twenty-five portholes offer an incredible view of space.

A man stands up and approaches you. You assume he is the captain.

"You have saved my life," you say as you extend your arm to shake hands. Instead of shaking your hand, he places a tiny wire across your forehead and hooks it around your ears.

"Now you will understand our language," says the man. "We have waited a long time for this."

You gasp when you realize that this man is not from Earth. He is an alien being.

"Come," the captain says. "Place your body in this Computerized Particle Decoder."

If you question the captain, turn to page 6.

If you refuse to enter the Particle Decoder, turn to page 9.

You are taken from your spacecraft into the gigantic mother ship. You walk down long corridors. Then you are put into a single-person elevator that whisks you upward. When the door opens, you look into a room that has five more people who are exact copies of the look-alikes.

"We've been expecting you," says one alien. He is wearing a badge on his uniform to distinguish him from the others.

"What is this!" you ask, appalled. "Why do you all look alike?"

"We are clones," says the man, "from Conwa."

"Clones? What are they?" you ask.

"We have been reproduced from the cell of one person," the man answers. "We've been searching for a new person to clone. And now we have one."

If you try to convince the man that you are not a good candidate for cloning, turn to page 23.

If you look around for a way to escape, turn to page 52.

When you enter the atmosphere of Planet X-24, the ship turns a fiery red and you are afraid that it might melt. But the heat decreases as you get closer to the planet, and the ship lands safely.

You step out of the craft and look around. In the distance you can see steam rising from a bubbling hot spring. To your left, you see a hill that appears to be made of ice.

If you investigate the hot spring, turn to page 8.

If you investigate the ice hill, turn to page 50.

"Hey," you say. "I'm just one person. I'm not worth cloning."

"Of course you are," the man says. "We're going to make ten other people who look exactly like you."

"I find it a horrible prospect," you answer.

"But why?"

"Because I am unique and I want to stay that way."

"We care nothing for uniqueness! 'In Uniformity Is Strength!' That is the motto of Conwa."

"How can you say that? Don't you care about individuality?" you ask.

"Care?" says the man, momentarily puzzled. "Oh, yes . . . that is a feeling. I've heard of feelings. But they are a thing of the past." He pauses for a moment and then says, "Strap yourself into the chair. We must prepare for landing on Conwa."

If you refuse, turn to page 15.

If you strap yourself into the chair, turn to page 43.

The officer holds the injector to your leg. You experience a hot, burning sensation as the serum enters your body.

At first you grow dizzy; then you feel as if you are floating. Horrified, you watch as your body begins to fade away, as if it is being broken up into trillions of electrons and neutrons. Your human consciousness remains for some time as you watch the officer frantically try to adjust the solution.

Then you hear him as he communicates with the Control Room.

"I am sorry, Captain. I cannot rearrange the Earthling's makeup. He is disintegrating into fundamental particles."

Those are the last words you hear.

The End

You have taken only three steps when a woman runs at you, threatening you with a stick. The others pick up stones and start to throw them in your direction.

You cannot bring yourself to use your laser against such primitive weapons, so you turn around and run.

You manage to elude your pursuers by running into a dense forest. Exhausted, you lean against a tree.

Suddenly, you hear a ferocious growl. Then, from out of the darkness, a mammoth cat-like creature leaps at you.

If you grab your laser and try to shoot, turn to page 61.

If you duck, turn to page 88.

You walk to the Particle Decoder and sit inside. It looks like a glass box surrounded by colored lights.

Once you are seated, an alien attaches you to seven electrodes. Then the lights begin to flash crazily. You feel yourself growing faint. Then you lose consciousness.

When you awaken, you are lying on a hard cot.

"Strange," says the medical officer. "You are made up of almost all hydrogen and oxygen," he says.

"Water," you say. He ignores you.

"I do not know if we can adjust your components to survive on Meson, our planet."

"Where is that?" you ask.

"In the Clivon Galaxy."

You watch as the medical officer prepares solutions to change your human body. You are horrified.

(continued on page 27)

"No!" you cry. "Don't change me!" You try to raise yourself from the table, but you can only move your arms. The rest of you is stuck to the surface.

"You cannot move until I release the electromagnetic bonds that bind you," the officer says. "So struggling is useless."

The officer then prepares a solution to be injected into you with a strange gun-like apparatus.

If you cooperate, turn to page 24.

If you try to grab the Particle Injector, turn to page 37.

Once again you are alone in space, grateful that you were able to escape.

You ask your computer for the location of the nearest planet. It gives you a choice.

If you want to go to Planet X-24, turn to page 21.

If you want to go to Planet Y3W, turn to page 35.

You get down on your hands and knees, but the lasers are coming so close to you that you lie down on the floor. Then you begin to crawl on your belly toward the laser fire that is coming from the darkness. You hope that the people fighting the robots are the aliens from the ship.

At least they are not machines, you think as you make your way across the enormous room.

Lasers whiz over you from both sides, but you keep on going. Finally, you reach the darkness.

"Fine job, Earthling," says the voice of the captain. "Had you stayed with the robots, you would have been doomed to a life of slavery. I commend your courage."

The End

Soon the siren stops. You wonder if the danger is over, but then the whizzing noises of shooting laser beams fill the air. You are afraid to open the door because you suspect that a full-scale battle is taking place in the corridor.

Without warning, three of the buttons by the side of the door begin to flash.

If you push the red button, turn to page 42.

If you push the yellow button, turn to page 70.

If you push the green button, turn to page 93.

Reluctantly, you walk away from the lake. Just then you hear a scream. You turn to look at the water and you see the head of a monstrous creature; its huge open jaws expose two rows of razor-sharp teeth.

Suddenly, you realize what the people were trying to tell you. You smile gratefully at them. They have saved your life.

The End

You are taken to a huge room.

"Here," says your guide, "we teach children how to behave like children. You see, they are all clones from adult models. They do not know how to be children. They have to be taught."

You are appalled. There are nine little boys who look exactly alike and twelve identical little girls. You listen to the teacher.

"This is a ball," the teacher says. "You roll it or throw it or play catch with it."

"Soon we will clone you," says the guide. "And the room will be filled with kindergartners who look exactly the way you did when you were a child."

(continued on page 33)

"Never!" you say. "Never, never, never!"

You race out of the building and jump onto the first monorail that you see. It takes you to the edge of a dark forest.

Turn to page 58.

"Why are you making that strange noise?" the alien asks you.

It takes you a few minutes to stop laughing before you can answer the question. Finally, you explain; he is amazed.

He asks you if you will stay on the planet for a while in order to lecture the beings of Brancusi about Earth civilizations.

You agree to stay for two months. You are a celebrity. When it is time to go home, the most learned scientist on Brancusi asks if she may accompany you back to Earth.

If you tell her that you do not want to take her with you, turn to page 82.

If you agree to take her, turn to page 117.

You set your coordinates in the direction of Y3W. Suddenly, you begin to slow down. You wonder what is happening, for you have done nothing to decrease velocity.

You look out the porthole and see a huge planet before you. You have heard of eccentric solar bodies, but you have never seen one. It is an awesome sight; for this planet is not round. Instead, it is shaped like a hamburger bun. Furthermore, it glitters, even from a great distance in space.

You prepare to enter the gravitational field and land on the planet. But, without any guidance, your ship goes into orbit around the planet instead.

Emergency! you think. *I have lost control of my spacecraft.*

Turn to page 48.

You step back and look up. You tremble when you realize that you are standing next to a gigantic beast that has the body of *Tyrannosaurus rex* and the head and trunk of a monstrous elephant. Its tusks are five feet long and its red eyes are glaring. Suddenly, the creature swings its trunk straight at you.

If you try to duck, turn to page 55.

If you jump to one side, turn to page 69.

You reach for the Particle Injector, but you are stopped.

"We are traveling at five times the speed of light at this very moment," says the medical officer. "Soon we will enter the Clivon Galaxy. If you have not been adjusted, you will not survive the alien atmosphere. You have no choice."

The officer moves toward you; then he places the Particle Injector against your leg.

You feel a warm, burning sensation that travels quickly throughout your entire body. You feel as if you are breaking apart. You look at your hands, but they are no longer there. You look down. Part of your body has disappeared.

The medical officer moves quickly. He injects 5 cc. of pro-particle solution into your disappearing body.

Turn to page 51.

"I would like to be refreshed," you answer.

"As you wish," says the alien.

You are taken on a conveyer belt to a building that is made entirely of glass and steel.

A robot approaches you. An arm-like manipulator reaches out and sprays you with a fine mist. Suddenly, you feel energetic and alert. You are amazed. "This is wonderful!" you say. "On Earth, if we are tired, we must sleep."

"Sleep . . ." says one of the beings. "We have heard myths in which beings must recline and remain perfectly still for hours. Could that be sleep?"

"Yes. That is sleep," you say. "What do you eat on this planet?" you ask.

"Eat?" says the alien.

"Food," you explain. "It fuels the body."

"There is no such thing here. The air we breathe provides all the fuel we require."

Then I will starve here! you think.

(continued on page 39)

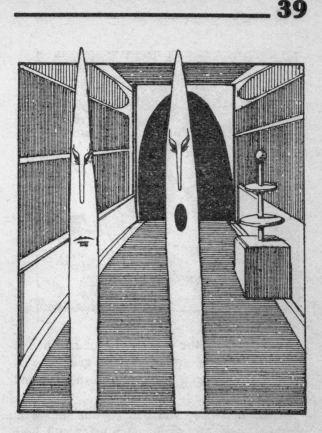

"In a special greenhouse, we have what we call prehistoric vegetation. Perhaps you could eat that," ventures the alien.

If you want to eat the prehistoric vegetation, turn to page 64.

If you do not want to risk eating strange food, turn to page 75.

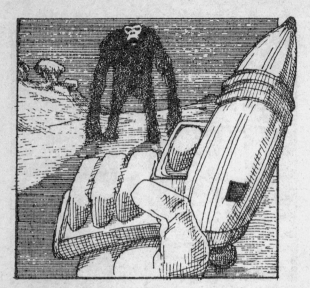

You climb up the side of the mountain; but when you reach the ledge, the giant ape is gone. You see huge footprints in the dirt and start to follow the tracks.

In the distance, you can see an ape. You remove your laser from its holster and take aim. Just as you are about to shoot, a huge hairy hand reaches out and cracks you on the head with a rock.

You've had it.

The End

Gleek looks at your vehicle with wonder. You motion to him to follow you. Inside the spacecraft, Gleek's eyes almost pop out of his head with surprise.

He reaches out to touch something.

"No!" you shout.

But it is too late. You blast off, with Gleek as your companion.

Turn to page 108.

Fearfully, you push the red button and wait. Nothing happens. Then you sniff the air.

A strange odor is seeping into the room. The more you breathe, the dizzier you feel. Finally you lose consciousness.

You are doomed.

The End

You sit in the chair and pull the strap over your chest. Then you watch as the spacecraft enters the Conwa atmosphere. Soon you have landed.

"Come," says the leader. "I will show you our laboratory. Or, if you prefer, I will show you the kindergarten first."

If you visit the kindergarten, turn to page 32.

If you go to the lab with the leader clone, turn to page 71.

You stand perfectly still and wait. A small child walks over to you. You squat down and smile. But you realize that she cannot see your face through the obstruction of the helmet.

You check the atmosphere-reading module on your belt and discover that the atmosphere on this strange planet is compatible with Earth's. Cautiously, you remove your helmet.

"Ahh! Ohh!" cry the people when they recognize a face vaguely similar to theirs.

Then the child reaches out and touches your cheek. You smile broadly. The child smiles, too.

You take a peppermint from your inside pocket and hand it to the child. You show her how to put it in her mouth. When she does, she shrieks with delight.

Just then, a huge boulder crashes into the valley from a ledge above.

(continued on page 45)

"Argh!" the people cry and they run into a nearby cave. You look up. There, on the ledge, stands an enormous ape. *Gigantopithecus!* you think.

If you go after the creature, turn to page 40.

If you run into the cave, turn to page 65.

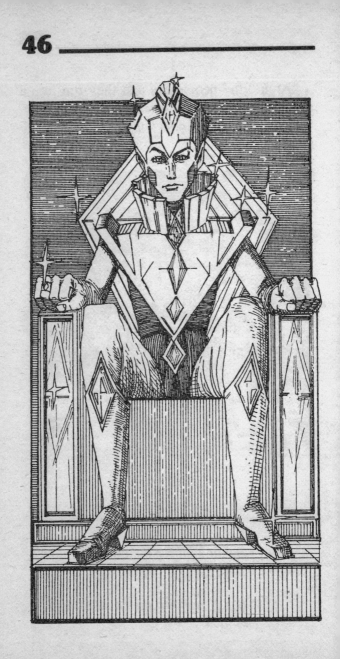

You walk with the captain through a long corridor that appears to be made of glass, but it is stronger and thicker than glass. You realize that you are walking in a crystal corridor. Then you enter a vast crystal room. Everything sparkles; everything shines.

In the center of the room, an alien sits on a crystal throne.

"Our mission is complete," the captain reports. "And, for the first time, we have returned with an Earthling."

The leader nods. "Did you encounter any robots?" he asks.

"None," the captain replies. Then he turns to you. "The robots, created years ago by one of our own, have turned on us. They are trying to take over our planet, and then they plan to attack Earth and enslave all the people. With your help, we are hoping to prevent this from happening. But it could be very dangerous. Will you help?"

If your answer is no, *turn to page 53.*

If your answer is yes, *turn to page 62.*

You attach your universal decoder to your communicator.

"Mayday! Mayday!! Do you read me?"

"Yes, I read you," answers a voice. "You are not in trouble. You have just come up against the anti-matter gravitational field that protects our planet. You will remain in orbit until we are ready for you."

You wait. In about three minutes your craft enters an opening in the anti-matter gravitational field, and you land on the planet.

You climb out of the craft and are approached by two forms. Their bodies are smooth and shiny and streamlined; their top comes to a point.

"Welcome to Brancusi," says one of the creatures. "From what planet do you come?"

"Earth, in the Milky Way Galaxy."

"We have never been visited by an Earthling before. You appear to be weary. Would you like to be refreshed before you tour our planet?"

If you would like to tour immediately, turn to page 12.

If you prefer refreshment first, turn to page 38.

This is it, you think. You start to run.

The darkness erupts with light as bright beams of lasers flash around you. You do not stop; you do not even think. You just keep on running until you reach the source of the lasers that are shooting at the robots.

"You made it," says the captain. "It was a risk. But you were successful."

You stay with the captain until his men have won the battle.

"Now," says the captain, "you must join us in a celebration. You will be our guest of honor. Then we will take you home."

The End

You walk toward the ice hill. You are amazed to see movement inside the hill. Dark spots change positions within, while the outside remains still.

You touch the surface. Instead of its being icy cold, it is slimy and warm.

Suddenly, the hill moves. To your horror, it raises itself slightly and covers you. Then you are sucked up inside. You have just been ingested by a giant amoeba.

The End

You watch as your body takes shape once more. It seems no different; and yet, your breathing seems slower, your eyesight clearer. Your body is functioning on a new level.

As you look out of the portholes, great waves of fire surround the ship.

"We have entered the Clivon atmosphere," the medical officer says. "There is no longer any need for you to wear your pressurized suit."

In minutes, you have landed. Then the captain approaches you.

"If you would like to go to your room and rest before seeing our planet, you may. Or you may come with me while I make my report."

If you go with the captain, turn to page 47.

If you go to your room, turn to page 78.

I don't have a moment to spare, you think as you start to run.

"Halt!" says one voice. "Halt!" says another. But you do not stop. Instead, you continue to run.

You burst through a door and come upon a spiral staircase. You jump on the rail and slide down to the bottom.

You land in the chamber that contains your spacecraft. Quickly, you climb inside.

I hope the doors open to let me out as easily as they let me in. Well, here's hoping, you think as you blast off.

The doors of the spaceship open just in time.

Turn to page 28.

"I don't think I am cut out to be a hero," you say sadly. "I am too frightened to risk my life."

"I understand," the captain says. "Any thinking and feeling creature would feel the same way. When confronted with a real threat, only a fool would not be afraid. Wisdom comes when you recognize the fear and then make the decision to act in spite of it. That is the way one learns and grows."

You think about what the captain has said. Finally, you reply. "I will try," you say. "That is the most I can do."

"It is all one creature can ask of another," the captain replies softly.

Turn to page 62.

You dive into the water. It is cold but refreshing. When you rise to the surface, the people are frantically beckoning to you. You think that perhaps they do not know how to swim and are therefore frightened by the water.

I'll show them, you think. You roll onto your back and begin to do a back stroke, proud that you can demonstrate this skill to them.

You are so involved in showing them how to swim that you do not see the gigantic prehistoric beast swimming toward you. That is, you do not see it until its huge, gaping mouth, lined with two rows of razor-sharp teeth, is poised above you. By then, it is too late.

The End

You duck. You can feel the trunk swing over your head. You look up just as the beast takes aim again.

You do not pay close attention to the rest of the animal. He lifts his huge foot.

Squish!

The End

You step outside. You look to your left and see nothing. Then you look to your right. You are shocked to see seven short, metallic robots coming down the corridor.

Turn to page 84.

Suddenly, you grip your side as if you are in pain. Then you pull your Impulse Molecule Destroyer from under your shirt.

"What is that?" you say, looking up at the sky.

Greegon looks up, too.

"Don't move," you say, "I've got you covered with my IMD."

"Don't shoot!" Greegon begs when she sees your weapon.

"The Earthling doesn't have to," says the voice of the captain as he emerges from behind a boulder. "You are ours now, Greegon," says the captain.

Then the captain turns to you. "That was very clever and very brave. Planet Earth may never know that it has been saved by you. But we know that you are a hero."

The End

You are lost and alone and you do not know what to do. You decide to enter the forest.

Then you hear the sound of someone crying. You follow the noise and come upon a young man who is sitting on the ground. His head is resting on his knees, and he is sobbing.

(continued on page 59)

"What's the matter?" you ask. "Why are you so sad?"

"I am sad because a friend of mine has chosen to return to Conwa and live with the clones. We have just said goodbye."

"What is so sad about living with clones?"

"A clone has no feelings. In Conwa, there is no love, no kindness, no caring. Life itself means nothing. Those of us who have escaped are originals. No one has ever been cloned from our cells. We still have our feelings."

"You mean there are more of you?" you ask.

"Many more. Would you like to meet them?"

"Oh, yes!"

"It is a dangerous journey. Very dangerous."

If you embark upon the journey, turn to page 76.

If you do not wish to take the risk, turn to page 95.

You start to run, zigzagging down the hall.
"You must stop, Earthling," says the voice.
But you pay no attention.
Zap! You should have listened.

The End

You pull your laser gun from its holster. But the saber-tooth tiger is quicker than you are.

The End

The captain continues. "We do not know whether we should attack the robots or try to locate the headquarters of their leader. You make the decision."

If you go after the robots, turn to page 107.

If you go after their leader, turn to page 113.

Now isn't the time to investigate something rough and rubbery, you think as you start to run. You don't even look back to see what it is.

All you want to do is find your spaceship and get off this planet. You see a hill ahead of you and think that if you climb up, you may be able to locate your vehicle.

You scamper up the hill and look around. Just as you think you spot your spacecraft, the hill begins to move.

Earthquake! you think.

If you lie down and cling to the shaking hill, turn to page 114.

If you try to slide down the hill, turn to page 116.

You are taken by a conveyer belt to the greenhouse. It is filled with lush, green plants. There is a table filled with seeds.

"These seeds were discovered in our archaeological expeditions," explains the alien. "They were preserved in ice for hundreds of millions of years. Our myths tell of plants that spring from seeds in dirt; and so we planted some seeds and they grew. But we do not know what these growths are used for."

You are amazed. The garden is filled with spinach and carrots, green beans, tomatoes, and lettuce.

"Perhaps," says the alien, "you can explain to us how these growing things are used."

You pull a carrot from the dirt, clean it off, and take a small bite.

You show them your teeth and how you chew food. Then you explain about how your body processes the food.

"Amazing," says one of your guides.

"You are a being from ancient times. Come, we will show you our museum."

Turn to page 80.

You huddle in the cave with the other people while huge rocks and boulders crash past the entrance. Finally, *Gigantopithecus* gives up his attack.

One by one, you cautiously emerge from the cave, fearful that the monstrous ape may be planning to ambush you once you are out in the open.

Finally, Gleek determines that it is safe, and he signals the group to follow him as he walks across the valley.

(continued on page 66)

You join the others as they run along the path.

Gleek stops on the far side of the valley, where a clear waterfall cascades into a small lake.

You watch as the people lie down on their stomachs and scoop the water into their mouths. You do the same, and you are grateful for the delicious and refreshing drink.

At that moment, more than anything, you want to dive into the water and clean yourself. It has been days since you bathed.

The group watches as you take off your clothes. Then, when you prepare to dive in, they begin to scream and tug at you.

Their interference frustrates you because you cannot explain to them what you are doing. You pantomime that you are going for a swim, but they continue to scream and pull at you.

If you give in to their protests and stay out of the water, turn to page 31.

If you defy them and dive into the water, turn to page 54.

You are afraid that you will make the alien very angry if you tell him; or, even worse, you might hurt his feelings. But you know that you will have a very funny story to tell when you return to Earth.

On your flight home, you laugh out loud as you think about the display case. And then you suddenly think: *I wonder if dinosaurs really looked like the reconstructions we see in our museums. After all, those models were also made from piles of bones.*

The End

You jump. You can feel the trunk whiz past your head. Then you grab hold of the tusk and swing onto it. The beast is enraged. He cannot swipe you away with his trunk no matter how hard he tries.

Well, at least I'm safe for the moment, you think, *although I certainly don't want to ride on this weird creature for very long.*

The monster becomes so furious that it starts to run toward a cluster of trees.

If you try to swing onto a branch, turn to page 99.

If you don't want to risk such a maneuver, turn to page 112.

You push the yellow button. Slowly, a panel on the door slides open and you can look out into the corridor. A battle is taking place between the aliens from the ship and a group of robots.

"There is the Earthling!" shouts the mechanical voice of a robot when he sees your face. "Get it!"

Turn to page 94.

You disembark from the spaceship and board a high-speed monorail. It takes you right to the entrance of the lab.

Inside, seven scientists who look exactly alike in their white coats are working feverishly over a series of test tubes.

"Ah," says one when he sees you. "Another candidate?"

"Precisely," says the leader clone.

"Come," the scientist says to you. "It won't hurt. We only require one cell."

He approaches you with a strange-looking instrument. It looks as if it could be a deadly weapon, and you wonder if he is lying.

If you think he is lying, turn to page 87.

If you think he is telling the truth, turn to page 97.

"Here," says the captain, handing you a small pen-like weapon. "Take this Impulse Molecule Destroyer and use it if you are in trouble. Now you must walk slowly out into the open so that Greegon can see you. That is the only way she will know that we are telling the truth."

Your knees are trembling, but you manage to make your legs work as you leave the safety of the vehicle and walk onto the flat land.

"Greegon!" the captain's voice booms. "See the Earthling!"

"Send it to me!" shouts a voice, "so that I may inspect it. Send it up the mountain."

You are horrified at the thought of going all alone to meet this evil leader. But, bravely, you begin to climb.

You climb for more than half an hour. Suddenly, a blinding light shines in your eyes.

"Halt, Earthling!" Greegon's voice booms.

Greegon rises from behind a huge boulder and walks toward you. She reaches out and pinches your arm.

(continued on page 73)

"Your covering is alien," Greegon says. "But it appears that you *are* an Earthling. You will be the leader of the conquering forces that will take over Planet Earth. Come with me."

If you go with Greegon, you are afraid that you will not be able to escape. You wonder if now is the time to use your Impulse Molecule Destroyer.

If you use your Impulse Molecule Destroyer, turn to page 57.

If you go with Greegon, turn to page 79.

"No!" you cry. "How would you like to be put in a cage?"

"He'll never know the difference," the man replies. "Now get out of my way before I use this laser on you."

Gleek senses that the man is threatening you. With one leap, he rushes at the man and knocks the laser out of his hand.

"Hooray!" Maria cries. "Hooray for Gleek! He's a hero!"

"Yes," you say quietly. "He *is* a hero and he deserves to be returned to his home. And that's what I'm going to do right now."

Gleek looks at you. His expression is filled with gratitude.

The End

"I thank you for your offer," you answer politely. "But I would be afraid to eat something that I do not know. However, I do have a question that I would like to ask you," you add.

"What is that?"

"Why is it that you have no arms and no hands? Are they not necessary?"

"Millions of years ago we evolved into this streamlined form," the alien answers. "When technology progressed to the point where robots could do everything for us, we no longer had any need for appendages. In our museum, however, we have made models of ancient beings similar to you. We constructed them from artifacts and skeletal forms that were discovered deep in the covering of our planet. Would you like to visit the museum?"

"Of course," you answer.

Turn to page 80.

"I would risk anything to meet the exiles," you say. "Let's be off."

You travel for two days through the living forest, where carnivorous plants reach out for you at unexpected moments. A fern almost grabs you, but the young man pulls you from its clutches and saves your life.

(continued on page 77)

When you arrive at the home of the exiles, they are overjoyed that someone new has joined them. You look around. Every face is different; every voice has a different tone. You even love the sound of people arguing.

When you explain to the group that you are from Earth, they are intrigued.

"Then we must do our best to travel to this place," says a woman scientist. "I shall start to design a spacecraft at once. It may take years, but we shall succeed."

Everyone cheers and there is a great celebration to commemorate the new venture.

You are especially comforted because you know there is a chance that someday you will return to Earth.

The End

You are taken underground, then down a long tunnel to the end of a corridor. The door to your room is made of shining metal. As soon as you enter, the door slams closed. You are alone.

Inside, the room is stark white, without any furniture. There is a red lever on one side of the door and a row of buttons on the other side. You push one button and a bed emerges from the wall. Another button turns on a light.

Suddenly a loud, shrieking siren blasts in the hallway outside your room.

If you think the siren is an alarm of danger, turn to page 30.

If you go outside to investigate the siren, turn to page 56.

You start to walk. Greegon is behind you, her laser gun trained on your back.

"Help!" you cry, as you pretend to trip on a rock and stumble to the ground.

"Rise up, Earthling," Greegon orders.

"I cannot," you say, holding onto your ankle, hoping to stall.

"Then you are no good to me," Greegon says as she points her laser and shoots.

The End

"This is the Brancusi Museum of Ancient Civilization," the alien says as you approach a huge glass building.

Inside, in hall after hall, there are glass and steel display cases. They are surrounded by miniature aliens.

"Those are our small beings. One day they will be my size," explains the alien.

Schoolchildren! you think. *Just like on Earth*.

"Here we have a model of ancient beings," says the alien. "We have constructed the model from skeletal remains."

"The ring around the being's neck is a ritual necklace worn by a chief, we believe. Note the shining indentation used for a bed. It even has some sort of communications system, as you can see from the primitive pipes that protrude from one end."

When you see the display, you are in such shock you cannot even speak. You listen while the alien continues.

Turn to page 105.

The path over the bridge is gentle. Since you do not like the looks of the forest, you cross the stream and walk for hours.

Finally, you are exhausted. You lie down to rest and close your eyes.

"Gotcha!" says one person as she grabs you.

"Gotcha!" says her look-alike with a grin.

"Gotcha!"

"Gotcha!"

"Gotcha!"

"Gotcha!"

"Gotcha!"

The End

You do not tell the scientist that you are uncomfortable with the idea of traveling with a strange creature on such a long journey.

Instead, you tell her that you cannot take her because the Earth's atmosphere would kill her. She protests, but you refuse to listen.

When you return to Earth, you tell everyone about your adventures. But they do not believe you because you have no proof.

I could have made a major contribution to science if I had brought her with me, you think. I missed the chance of a lifetime because I was afraid of being with somebody different. That was a huge mistake.

The End

You jump from the platform onto the floor. *I was almost a human sandwich,* you think with relief.

You stand up. Just then, the door bursts open and you are confronted by a robot holding a laser weapon.

"You are our prisoner, Earthling," says the robot. "Soon you will be our slave."

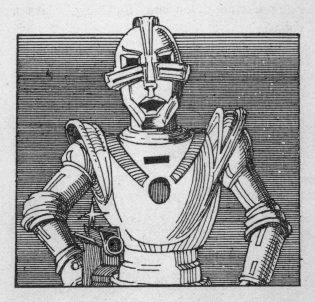

The End

You start to duck back into the room, but the arm of the lead robot points directly at you, and a red light begins to flash.

"Stay where you are, Earthling," says a voice.

If you try to run, turn to page 60.

If you do as the robot says, turn to page 101.

You open the door. Blinding beams of light flash past you. The battle is raging from all directions.

Aiming your metal disintegrator at the first phalanx of robots, you pull the trigger. A great whooshing noise erupts from your gun as the lethal beams flash toward the robots.

You watch, expecting the metal enemies to disintegrate before your eyes. But nothing happens. The robots are not affected by your weapon.

"You have made a great mistake, Earthling," says one of the robots as he advances toward you with five of his soldiers. "We are made of high-density plastic, not metal."

A blinding flash of light erupts from the robot. It is the last sight of your life.

The End

"I can't let you do this!" you say, moving toward the man.

He raises his laser to shoot.

"No!" Maria cries. "Don't shoot!" And with a swift movement of her little arm, she knocks the laser out of the man's hand. Immediately, you pick it up.

"Now," you say. "Don't move until I get Gleek out of here."

You reach over and take Gleek by the hand. "Come," you say. "I'm taking you home."

The End

You strongly suspect that the scientist is lying. You watch as he approaches you.

With one swift movement, the scientist pulls a trigger. A dart-like apparatus shoots out and grazes your arm.

"There," says the scientist. "It didn't hurt at all, did it? It's such a painless way to obtain a cell sample."

Soon you are surrounded by ten other miniature *you*'s.

The End

You duck. The animal leaps over your body. You turn and discover that you are facing an enormous saber-tooth tiger. Still, you do not want to use your laser. It seems wrong to kill such a magnificent animal with a laser gun.

Instead, you pick up a huge branch and swing it wildly in front of you. At the same time, you scream at the top of your lungs. To your great relief, the tiger stands a moment and looks at you, then it bounds off into the forest.

You are pleased that you were able to defend yourself against such a frightening creature. You are so pleased, in fact, you do not watch where you are walking.

(continued on page 89)

As you pass under a huge tree, you think you see a branch hanging in your path and you reach up to push it aside.

Oops! Your mistake. It was a thirty-foot-long python!

The End

You wait as the battle rages outside your door.

"Find the Earthling!" shouts a voice. "He is in one of these rooms!"

Horrified of being caught by robots, you lie on the bed and utilize your astronaut training. Concentrating hard, you use the powers of your mind to slow down your pulse and your breathing.

The door bursts open. But you do not move.

"Too late," says a robot as he leans over to inspect you. "The Earthling is dead."

(continued on page 91)

You listen as they leave the room. Still, you do not move.

Soon you hear the voice of the captain. "Earthling?" he asks. "Are you living?"

"Yes," you answer with a smile.

"You are very clever," says the captain. "You have foiled an enemy with the power of your mind instead of the force of a weapon. Obviously, we can learn from you. You may stay with us as long as you wish. Then, when you are ready, we will take you home again."

The End

Carefully, you back into the elevator, out of the line of fire. The battle lasts for almost half an hour.

Finally, you hear a robot voice say, "Retreat!" And, to your horror, three robots who have survived the battle back into the elevator.

The door closes. In a jerky movement, one robot turns toward you, its laser arm extended.

"Ah," it says. "The Earthling is still with us. What every robot needs is an Earthling to do its work. You will do just fine."

The End

You push the green button. A table and two chairs rise out of the floor. You can still hear the battle raging outside your door.

"Where is the Earthling?" asks a strange mechanical voice. It is the voice of a robot.

In a panic, you turn to the panel and push a purple button.

The section of floor on which you are standing begins to rise. Higher and higher you go. *I'll be crushed when I get to the ceiling,* you think.

Suddenly there is a loud pounding on the door.

If you jump off the platform, turn to page 83.

If you think the platform may be a way out, turn to page 102.

In a panic, you duck to the side. Then slowly you reach up and slide the panel closed. Your heart is pounding and your hands are trembling. You are terrified.

You try to calm down by taking slow, deep breaths, knowing that if you cannot think clearly, you will not be able to save yourself.

When you are calm, you consider your options.

If you connect the metal-disintegrator unit to your laser gun so that you can destroy the robots, turn to page 85.

If you think you can utilize your astronaut training in order to save yourself, turn to page 90.

"How dangerous is it?" you ask.

"In order to get there we must travel through the vicious forest."

"Vicious forest? What is that?"

"Many of the plants are carnivorous. They eat animals, including us."

The thought of being eaten by a plant is too overwhelming to you.

"I think I will stay here," you say, "close to the border."

The young man bids you a sad farewell.

One month later, you wonder if you should have traveled with him. This place is lonely, lonelier than anything you have ever known before. And now it is your home.

The End

You are so frightened that you do not move.

"This is your only chance, Earthling!" calls the voice from the dark. But you are too scared to run.

Suddenly, a burst of light flashes from the darkness. Then another and another.

You are caught in a full-scale laser battle.

If you get down on your hands and knees, turn to page 29.

If you seek shelter by moving back into the elevator, turn to page 92.

He probably is telling the truth, you think. *But I still don't want him to make other* me's.

As the scientist approaches, you kick out with your foot and knock the instrument from his hand.

"So," says the scientist. "You're one of those! Take this Earthling away!" he orders.

One of the other scientists grabs you and pulls you out the door. You are taken aboard the monorail and transported outside the boundaries of Conwa. Then you are pushed out of the car.

"You are exiled!" the scientist shouts before riding away.

Frightened, you look around.

Before you is a dark forest. To the right of the forest is a stream with a bridge running over it.

If you walk toward the forest, turn to page 58.

If you cross the bridge, turn to page 81.

You travel for two weeks, but you pass nothing.

"I fear," you say, "that we are traveling toward the edge of the universe."

"If that is the case," she answers, "then we will have a chance to test my theory that there *is* no end to the universe; that, at its edge, space merely doubles back on itself."

"Ah, that is a theory we have on Earth as well. I hope we are both right."

As a scientist, you know that you should have confidence in the theory. But a part of you believes that you will fall off the edge of the universe into nothingness.

The End

As the monster passes under a tree, you reach up and swing onto a vertical branch. The monster runs on.

Whew! you think. *I'm safe.*

Just as you take a deep breath, the branch begins to rise up from the ground. You have grabbed the leg of a *Pteranodon* and now you are flying through the air.

As the creature's huge wings flap rhythmically, you feel yourself beginning to lose your grip. You look down. Unfortunately, you fall just as the prehistoric bird is flying directly over a lake of bubbling acid.

Snap! Crackle! Pop!

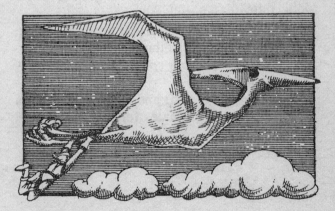

The End

Oh, no! It's an armadillo, you think. *A gigantic armadillo!*

Just then, the creature starts to roll up into a ball. Luckily, you roll onto the ground.

When you hit the dirt, you keep on rolling, right out of the path of the beast. You are overjoyed to see that your spacecraft is only a few feet ahead.

You run to the craft and climb inside. Then you set your coordinates for home and blast off.

There really is *no place like home*, you think.

The End

You stand perfectly still, afraid of what might happen if you move.

"Come with us," the robot says. Immediately, you are surrounded by robots. They take you down the corridor and then into an elevator. Down, down you move at an incredible speed. Then the elevator stops.

The door opens, and you step outside, still surrounded by robots.

"Run, Earthling!" cries a voice from the dark.

"Stay where you are," the robot says.

If you run toward the voice in the dark, turn to page 49.

If you prefer to take your chances with the robots, turn to page 96.

I made a mistake, you think, as you scrunch down on the platform to avoid being crushed.

When your head is only three inches from the ceiling, a panel opens and you are lifted into the room above.

But you do not stop there. Room by room, you rise to the surface of the planet. When you reach the top, the aliens are waiting.

"Welcome, Earthling," one of the aliens says. "That was a wise decision. You just avoided being caught by the robots. If that happened, you would never have been heard from again."

The End

Maria is taken, protesting, from the room. *I should have objected,* you think. But it's too late now.

Just then there is a sudden rumble and the entire space station begins to shake dangerously.

"We're going through an anti-matter zone!" one of the scientists cries in fear.

You look up. The wall of computers as tall as the room is being shaken loose. If it falls, everyone will be crushed.

Gleek sees this, too. Immediately, he runs to the wall and places his back against it, bracing it firmly with his powerful body until the shaking stops.

"Gleek saved us," says the man who thought Gleek was so disgusting only moments before. "A hero deserves to be taken home."

"That is exactly what I intend to do," you reply as you hug Gleek.

The End

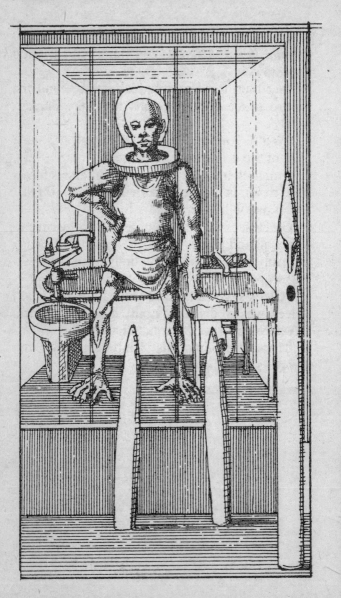

"Note, if you will, the headcovering on the chief," the alien says. "The throne also matches the sleeping apparatus. We assume that the chief stood inside the throne when making proclamations. The ritual altar also has a communications system similar to that of the bed."

You cannot stand this for another moment. You stare at the figure of the chief in the display case and burst out laughing.

The being in the case, reconstructed from human bones, is put together all wrong. The legs are where the arms should be. And he is standing on his hands.

The "ritual necklace" is a toilet seat, and the headdress is the lid. The bed is a bathtub, the altar, a sink.

Obviously, the archaeologists found some skeletal remains in an ancient Earth-type bathroom!

If you tell the alien that this is a horrendous mistake, turn to page 34.

If you do not wish to offend the alien, turn to page 67.

You hold on tightly. There are so many creatures in the cave that you are afraid you will be crushed if you get off.

You watch as one of the beasts lumbers toward you. With one swift movement of its trunk, it reaches out and grabs you.

You are a tasty snack.

The End

"We know that the robots are hidden in the depths of our planet. If we take you to one of our underground chambers, they will most likely sense you are there. When they show themselves, we will be ready."

Turn to page 78.

You are about to return Gleek to his planet when you pick up a signal from an Earth space station. You know that you cannot risk losing the signal by returning Gleek, so you set your coordinates for the station, thinking that this would be a good opportunity for Earth scientists to investigate early man.

After soaring through space for several hours, you sight the station. You signal to it, and then prepare to dock.

At first you are greeted warmly by the engineers in the station. But when they see Gleek, they are shocked.

"Whew!" says one of the men, holding his nose. "I bet he hasn't had a bath in his entire life! He's filthy!"

Uncomprehending, Gleek looks at the man and smiles.

(continued on page 109)

"He's no more than an ape!" another man says. "Just look at him . . . disgusting!"

Gleek seems hurt by the tone of voice that the man uses.

Just then, a child enters the room. "Oh!" she says with a smile. "He's wonderful!"

"Would you look at that?" a man says. "Maria hasn't smiled in weeks, she's been so lonely on this station. Now look at her!"

Maria runs over to Gleek and starts to hug him.

"No!" says one of the engineers. "Don't touch him! Get her out of here."

If you allow Maria to be taken from the room, turn to page 103.

If you tell the man that Gleek is gentle, turn to page 115.

You jump off the tusk. To your astonishment, the movement frightens the beasts and they back away in fear. You race through the exit.

In the distance, you see your spacecraft. *This is the most welcome sight I have ever seen in my entire life,* you think. *I've had enough adventure. I'm going home!*

The End

You travel in that direction for two months. But you do not pass one planet on which you can land.

You can only hope that you find a planet before your food supply runs out.

The End

The beast continues to run with you on its
tusk until it comes to a huge cave. The creature
dashes through the entrance. To your horror,
there are five similar beasts waiting inside.

Oh, no! you think. *I'm in the monster's lair.
I can't believe it!*

*If you think that the safest strategy
is to remain on the tusk, turn to
page 106.*

*If you leap off the tusk and risk
running through the herd to the exit,
turn to page 110.*

"We know that our treacherous sister directs her robots from the Platon Peaks on the far side of the planet. If we can discover her headquarters, we can destroy her. Come with us."

You board a cigar-shaped vehicle that rides on a track of air. In minutes, you, the captain, and a squadron of soldiers have reached the peaks. They rise from the surface of the planet in majestic splendor.

You stop at the base of the highest mountain. Quietly, the soldiers disembark and take cover. Then the captain takes out a tiny microphone.

"Hear me, Greegon," the captain says. "I have an Earthling."

The captain's voice is magnified one thousand times. His words resound in the valleys and the mountains.

Turn to page 72.

You lie down and hold on tightly. But the hill does not just shake back and forth; it moves forward! Then you notice that you are holding on to a kind of bony shell.

Oh, no! you think. *I'm riding on some sort of weird creature.*

If you think that it is an armadillo, turn to page 100.

If you think that it is a lizard, turn to page 118.

"Please!" you say. "Gleek is gentle. He wouldn't hurt Maria."

"Are you kidding?" the man says. "This ape belongs in a cage."

"He belongs on his own planet," you reply firmly. "And I will take him there as soon as I calculate the coordinates."

"Not on your life! We're taking him to Earth. He's a great specimen."

Gleek looks at Maria and smiles. He indicates through sign language that he has a child just her age. A big tear rolls down his cheek, and you know that he is frightened and homesick.

"You can't take him!" you say.

"You're wrong," the man says, pulling his laser and pointing it at you.

If you try to talk reasonably with the man, turn to page 74.

If you think the man is dangerous and you try to knock the gun from his hand, turn to page 86.

You slide down the hill. The ride is bumpier than you thought it would be. When you look back, you realize that you have been sliding on the back of a gigantic armadillo!

Convinced now that you are in a dangerous land of overgrown creatures, you resolve to get back to your spacecraft. The trouble is, you cannot find it. *I'm lost in a land of monsters,* you think.

Then you look up. Hovering overhead, with the Earth insignia painted on it, is a search-and-rescue craft. You wave frantically, and the craft lands just one hundred yards away.

You run toward it and the door opens. When you are inside, you are greeted enthusiastically.

"I'm glad we found you," says an astronaut. She smiles then, and adds: "Welcome home. We'll be there in no time."

The End

For many days, you and the scientist prepare for the journey back to Earth.

The flight begins normally; but on the third week out, your navigational system breaks down. Neither you nor the scientist can repair it, and you do not know where you are.

Finally, you both determine that the way to Earth is in one of two directions. You do not know which one to choose.

If you move 5 degrees to the left, turn to page 98.

If you move 32 degrees to the right, turn to page 111.

It's a prehistoric lizard, you think, just as the monstrous armadillo's snout swings around and sucks you inside.

The End